Special Message

_____

_____

_____

_____

_____

_____

It's Christmas Eve, and all is well.
The moonlit sky is clear.

Lukas

knows it won't be long till Christmas Day is here.

Santa and his reindeer friends are traveling around the world.

Lukas

hopes he's got a gift for every boy and girl.

Lukas

**made a careful list of lots of different things.
And cannot wait till morning comes
to see what Santa brings.**

There are cookies by the fireplace
and some milk for him to sip.
"That's just in case," LUKAS says,
"he's thirsty on his trip."

FOR SANTA

Stockings hang beside the fire that's glowing warm and bright.
A tall and sparkling Christmas tree is strung with fairy lights.

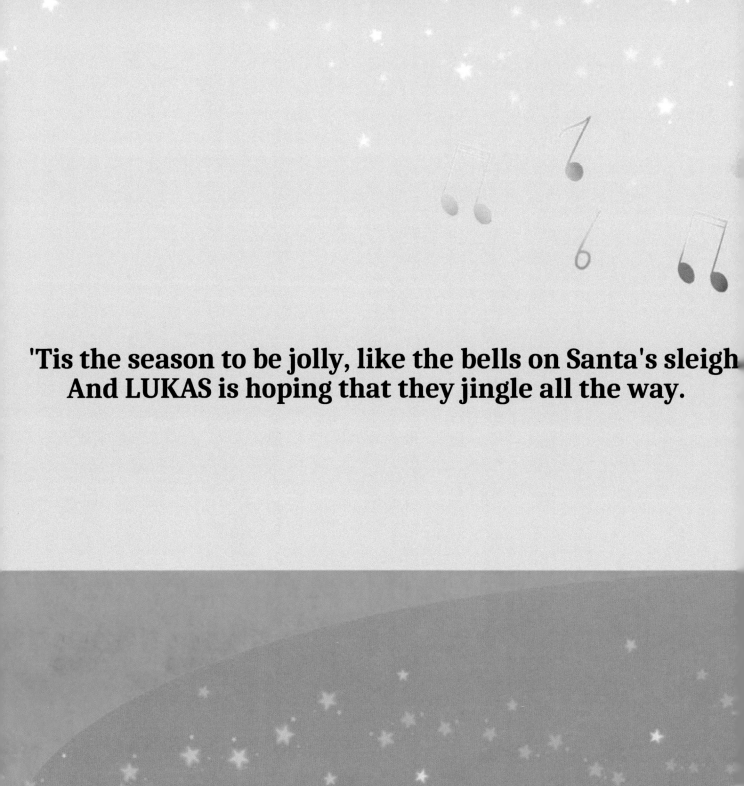

'Tis the season to be jolly, like the bells on Santa's sleigh
And LUKAS is hoping that they jingle all the way.

LUKAS wakes up early,
and rushes down the stairs.
And underneath the Christmas tree
are presents everywhere.

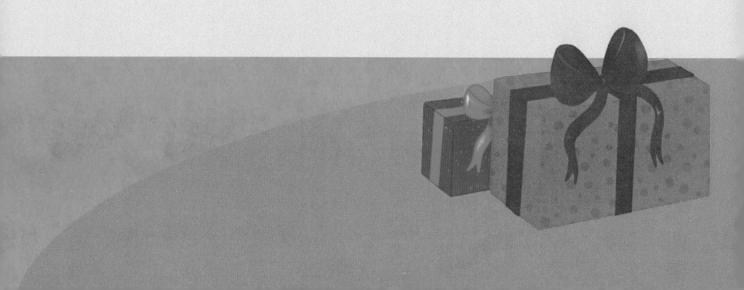

There are brightly colored boxes
with their ribbons and their bows.
And the smile upon LUKAS's face
just simply grows and grows.

LUKAS can hardly wait to see what's there inside.
And so, with grown-ups looking on,
the ribbons are untied.

LUKAS loves the holidays,
which come around each year,
a chance for you to celebrate
with those you hold most dear.

LUKAS's home is colorful with tons of decorations!

LUKAS's
always pleased to see their happy,
smiling faces.
As aunts and uncles, cousins too, arrive
from different places.

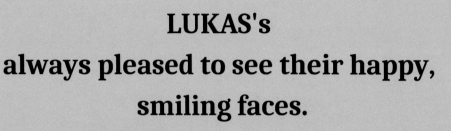

The house is full of lovely smells
from meats and sweets and treats.
LUKAS can't believe it.
There's so much there to eat.

LUKAS snacks on this and that,
then eats a little more.

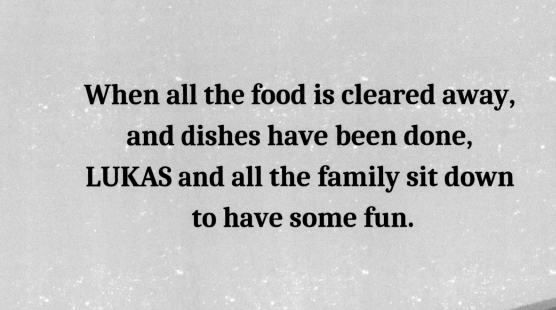

When all the food is cleared away,
and dishes have been done,
LUKAS and all the family sit down
to have some fun.

They play some board games,
cards as well, and make a lot of noise.
LUKAS watches cartoon shows
or maybe plays with toys.

They'll sing some Christmas carols
at the piano in the lounge,
till LUKAS's eyes get heavy
as the day is winding down.

Outside, the stars are twinkling,
and the snow is lying deep.
And gently, on that silent night,
LUKAS falls asleep.

The end

Made in the USA
Las Vegas, NV
18 December 2024

14815271R00026